# Her Phantoms

## 8 Horror Images

## and Vignettes

## of

## Horror Project Phantoms

# Her Phantoms

8   Horror Images

and Vignettes

of   Horror Project Phantoms

based on
Gaston Leroux's
The Phantom of the Opera

## the artist_AwayNowe

# Table of Contents

# Her  Phantoms

## 8 Horror Images

### and  **Vignettes**

of    Horror Project Phantoms

based upon

Gaston Leroux's

 Phantom of the Opera

by

**the artist_ awayNowe**

# Vignette 1

of

# Her Phantoms

# Despair Only

And yet I continue

Into What

Those hands

forever groping

And theirs not mine

Idiotic I feel

Playing their games

But if I don't

Out onto the street I go

And Into What

# Despair Only

And yet I continue

To smile

    To preen

        To perform for

But never myself

Never myself

    Am I with them

        Or for them

I hate all of these

    and myself

    But where to go

    There is nowhere else

Is this is what

is for me

Until I am old and gray

and well worn

from them

And cast aside

into the rubbish bin

of after thoughts

cast aside

for a new batch

of youths to

be put upon

I see those older ones

who clean around us young ones

They were like us before
And now they struggle
   continue to struggle
      as they struggled before

Abandoned
Because of their wrinkles
Because of their graying hair

Left without means
      to live upon

# Despair Only

And yet I continue

And I know

What Into

# Vignette 2

## Of

## Her Phantoms

# How can I sing

When all I want

is to **scream**


Instead I smile

and curtsey politely

For My Adoring Patrons

Who cant wait

to get me all alone

with them later tonight

When they bring me flowers

and flower me with compliments

For My Flower


Until at the final minute

My manager comes to

my rescue

To whisk me away

For another round

of chasing my flower

for another day

So are my days

    My prancing and singing

        For My Adoring Patrons


And my manager


    Better this

        Than the street

        The older ones always say

We all know

The young and the old

We all know

There are worst ways to exist
            than this
I am fed, I am clothed
        I have employment
                and small savings
        I have shelter
        that so many others do not


I am one of the lucky ones
I should feel grateful

But I do not

All I want is to

scream

# Vignette 3
## Of
## Her Phantoms

# I was gifted

        with beauty

     and a little song

     and placed into

     protective arms

I practiced day and night

      And beamed with pride

      when bestowed with
compliments

# And frightened

        When not

So young

    So frail

        So eager


For a chance

How naïve I was

To listen to

    the fairy tales


But Better this

    Instead of

But Better this

    I do not even
    want to think of

As long as I remain
    young and fresh and beauty
As long as I remain
    I can endure
My Men
    I can keep mostly clean
My Men
    I can keep with Them

Their Riches
    Help me succeed
even when their hands
        touch too much

# My Men

Love sweet for me

And I love sweet for Them


The gowns

the jewels

the food

The parties

the wine


my own bed to sleep

warm in

I practice day and night
for this
I practice day and night


# For My Men

# Vignette 4

## Of

## Her Phantoms

# My Men

I dance for

## My Men

I sing for

## Their Needs

## Their Wants

### Are Mine

## Their Needs

## Their Wants

Are Mine

to be sweet for


How affectionate

And teasing must I be

In order to barely make a living

My Hopelessness

and Distraught

I must always hide

Behind the smiles

of my

made up face

Behind all this

false glamor

My Men

Love to taste

My Men

Im Lucky

that they have

expensive taste

My Men

Im Lucky

that their hands

enjoy roaming

over me


Im Lucky

to be so well cared for


My Men

Their Needs

Their Wants

I can not even imagine

doing without


I would be even more
Hopeless Without

# My Men

I dance for

I sing for

# My Men

I cherish

# My Men

I cannot do

Without

My Men

    PLEAse do not

    Leave Me

    cold and hungry

    in the dark

My Men

    PLEAse do not

    Push Me

    into an even more

    punishing existence

# My Men

as hopeless as I am

With You

# My Men

I am

even more hopeless

Without You

# My Men

I can curl up with you

and at least pretend

I am safe

# My Men

I pretend Love

for you

as You pretend Love

for me

# My Men

## PLEAse
## Do Not Leave Me

How would I survive

How would I not starve

# My Men

## PLEAse
## Do Not Leave Me

I will still dance for you

I will still sing for you

# Vignette 5

## Of

## Her Phantoms

I must do Better

He says

I must smile Brighter

He says

I must look Beauty

He says


How am I not doing this

How should I do this

I plead


My Manager

Please Teach Me

How To Please

How Would You Like Me

How Should I Be

    For You

especially you

    For My Adoring Patrons

especially you

    For The Glamorous Crowd

especially you


You must be Fed too

With the Hard Work you do

    For Me

    For Me

This is why you do

For if I am out on the street

Than so are you

You have no more hope than I

I know thats why

you  threaten me    always

so I stay with you

instead of finding another

to     manage        Me

        For My Men

I Promise

My Manager

To do Better

Brighter

Beauty

I Promise

I can not have you starve

If you do

So do the other Beauties

We would all starve

Without You

To manage us

For

All Our Men

Our Adoring Patrons

Whose hands and lips
must be Fed

with Our Touches and Kisses

Whose wrinkled brows
and rough skin
must be Comforted

with Our Touches and Kisses

Our Adoring Patrons

must have Our Teases

Our Smiles

Our Admirations


Or what would their lives be without


My Manager

Please Teach Me

How To Please

# Vignette 6
## Of
## Her Phantoms

A glass of Wine Here
        A glass of Wine There

A glass of Wine
        He has spilled on my gown
                        His Gown
I must take my gown off
        His Gown off


So that he can wipe the wine off
my skin
So that he can clean me with
his hands


And I lovingly oblige

Kiss him sweet

as he removes my gown

His Gown

Kiss him sweet

as he cleans my skin

His Skin

Kiss him sweet

as he my

His

Kiss him sweet

as he my

His

A glass of Wine Here
  A glass of Wine There

Until Almost
Until Almost

He smiles
and I smile for him
He smiles
until He smiles
no more
and I still smile for him

Not wanting him to see
my nervousness
my hopelessness

He smiles no more

And now

insists upon more


insists upon too much more


and no where is
    my manager to save me


I smile
    and tease his hands
    to other parts of my body
I try to please him
    with my hands

But now his eyes are cold
as his smile is gone
and his hands
have become rough
and hard

My Adoring Patron
has had enough
has spent enough

and now needs

wants more


And

I must lovingly oblige

him

I kiss him sweet

         as he    my

                His

I kiss him sweet

         as he    my

                His

I kiss him sweet

         as he    my

                His

I kiss him sweet

         as he    my

                His

I kiss him sweet

My Adoring Patron
cradles me
in his arms

He kisses me sweet now
He kisses my tears
lovingly

He smiles
and I smile for him

He kisses me sweet now
He kisses my bruises
lovingly

My Adoring Patron
cradles me
in his arms

# Vignette 7
## Of
## Her Phantoms

# The Balcony

And into the

Nights Fresh Air


My Corset

Is too tight

To breathe a full breath

As I gasp

For more air


too many hands      tonight

too many waltzes    tonight

too many kisses     tonight

The Wine
  The Gown
    The Jewels
All Too Heavy
  Upon My Soul
All Too Heavy
  Of Whats left of It


I gasp for more air
  and eventually
    settle my nerves

I need to return

    for more hands

        more waltzes

        more kisses


I need to return

    for more recent

    Adoring Patrons


I need to return

I need to smile

    And not scream


I need to return

And endure the demeans

Just a few more hours
then I can sleep alone
warm in my own bed
with my stomach full
with roof over my head
Just a few more hours

I can stand
I can smile
I can preen
I can dance
I can sing

I hold onto
      Not Dreams
But my own Bed
And by me Fed

I hold onto
      Not Dreams
But Survival Instead


Although
    I do think
      about The Balcony

Leaving instead through the

gilded double doors

Leaving instead

**The Other Way**

**A Way With No Return**

I do think

about **The Balcony**

Lately

Alot

I think

   about the last

      I would feel

in the cool

      Nights Air

Washing Over Me

Comforting Me


      As I Fall

I wonder

    Would I Scream

    or

    Would I Smile

    Would I Genuinely

        Smile

      As I Fall

Away from all this
hopelessness

I wonder

I take another breath
of cool night air
As I wonder
As I return
Away from

My Balcony

# Vignette 8

## Of

## Her  Phantoms

Oh you would do nicely

My New Adoring Patron
            slowly words
with an underlying menace

the hairs on My Neck
                stand out
as his hands on My Neck
        caress harder

He thanks my manager
for this

young and
fresh and
beauty

My New Adoring Patron
  guides me to an alcove
  a little too far
  from the rest


And with a hand still hard
    on My Neck
roughly caresses My Breasts

I smile Brightly
    as I have been Taught
I cozy up close
    to him
and moan softly
    as I have been Taught

Even though I am shaking
    deep inside
    from fear

I am terrified
of this obvious monster
I am not safe from

Oh
I can not wait to have
    you alone and all
to myself

My New Adoring Patron
       slowly words
with an underlying menace

And murderous eyes
And I still smile
   and kiss him sweet

   as I was Taught

I still smile
   with his hand hard
     on My Neck
I kiss him sweet
   with his hand rough
     on My Breasts

I still smile

I kiss him sweet

Author Bio

No

Just enjoy

the images and

writings

For nowe

Made in the USA
Columbia, SC
02 August 2023

21134854R00057